New Hope

by PJ Gray

SADDLEBACK
EDUCATIONAL PUBLISHING
www.sdlback.com

ISBN-13: 978-1-68021-132-0
ISBN-10: 1-68021-132-3
eBook: 978-1-63078-465-2

Printed in Guangzhou, China
NOR/1115/CA21501590

20 19 18 17 16   1 2 3 4 5

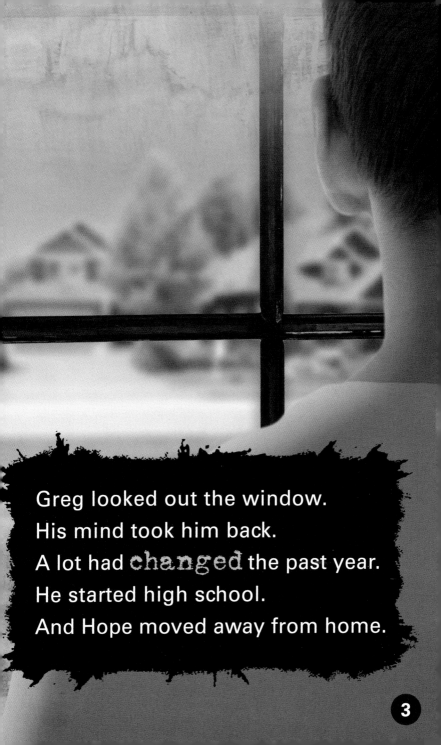

Greg looked out the window.
His mind took him back.
A lot had changed the past year.
He started high school.
And Hope moved away from home.

Hope was his older sister.
They were good friends too.
Hope played sports in school.
She was on many teams.
Her best sport was baseball.

Hope showed Greg how to throw a ball. They would go to the backyard. Throw and catch a baseball with each other. It was their time to talk and share.

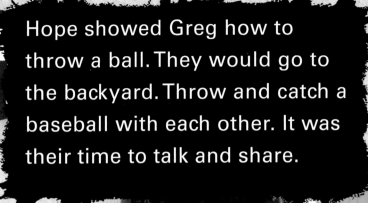

But then Hope graduated.
She joined the army.
Her unit was sent overseas.
She went to fight in a war.

Greg missed Hope.
He missed their time together.

Greg waited at the window.
His mom and dad would be
home soon. They went to get
Hope.

She was in a clinic. The
clinic was nine hours away.
She had been there seven
months. She was in two
hospitals before that.

Greg's mind took him back. Hope won an award at school. She was named Player of the Year.

Her coach shook her hand.
The crowd cheered.
Greg's mom took pictures.
Greg's dad wiped tears from
his eyes.

Now all that was gone.
It was in the past.

Greg waited for his parents.
Hope would be with them.
She was coming home.

But Greg did not know if she
would be the same person.

Hope had gone to war.
She liked being in the army.
She told Greg she felt proud.
She was doing her duty.

She didn't call home much.
She couldn't. But they spoke
on the phone once.

"I'll be home soon," Hope said. "We'll toss a few in the backyard."

"I still have your glove," Greg said.

"Good," she replied. "Take care of it for me."

15

Greg got the news three months later. A bomb blew up near Hope. She was hit. Hope was hurt. She was hurt bad. Others near her had died.

Greg's mind took him back to that day. He came home from school. His mom was crying.

His dad sat him down.
He told Greg the news.
"She is still alive. That's all
we know."

More news came later.
Hope was in an army hospital.
She was in a coma.

"Is she in the States?" Greg asked.

"No," his dad said. "Not yet. She
has to get better first. Then they
can move her."

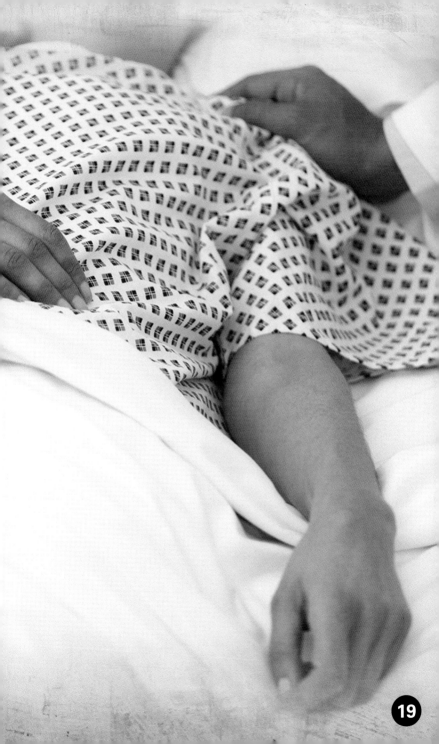

19

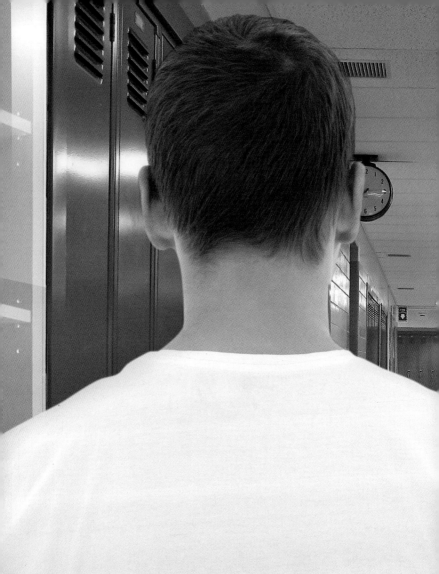

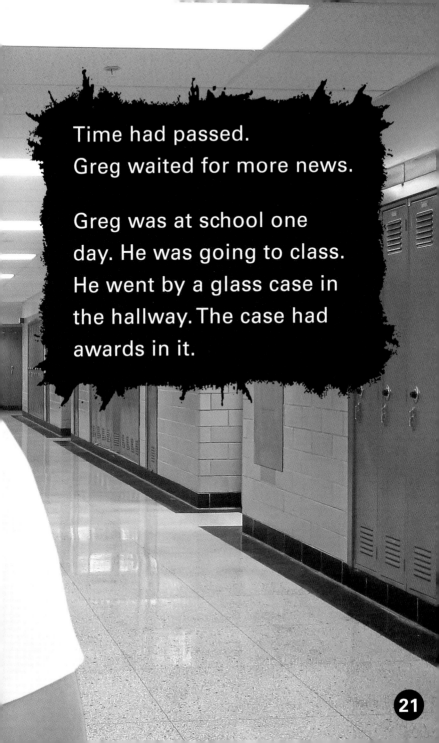

Time had passed.
Greg waited for more news.

Greg was at school one
day. He was going to class.
He went by a glass case in
the hallway. The case had
awards in it.

Greg looked at all of them.
One stood out.
It was a sports medal.
A medal Hope had won.

She ran a mile-long race.
She won first place.
That was not all.
Her time beat the
state record.

VARSITY
VOLLEYBALL
CHAMPIONS

Greg looked at the medal.
A friend came up to Greg.
"I heard about your sister,"
he said.

Greg did not speak.

"How is she?"

Greg slowly shook his head.
"We don't know."

"Sorry. Hey! Baseball starts soon. Are you going to try out?"

"I don't know," Greg said. "I've got to go."

Greg could not think about baseball. It made him think of Hope.

More time went by. Greg came home from school one day. His mom sat him down. She had news about Hope.

Hope was back in the States. She was in a new hospital. His sister was out of the coma. She was getting better.

"One more thing," his mom said. She began to cry.

"What?" Greg asked.

"Her leg," his mom said. "She lost part of it. She will never run again."

Greg was in shock. He shook his head. "Are you sure?"

His mom nodded.

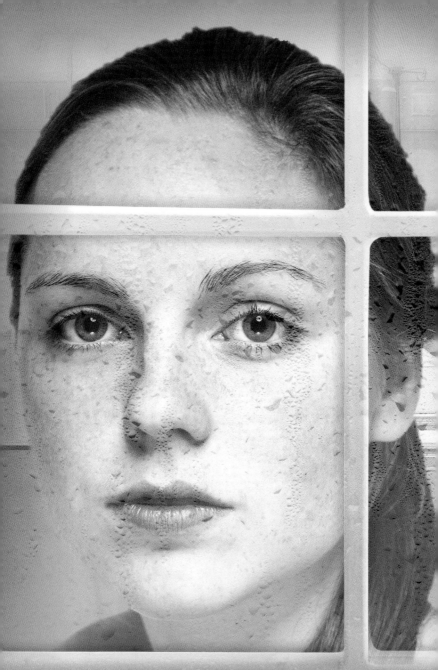

"Did you talk to her?"
Greg asked.

"No. The doctors told us."

"When can we talk to her?"
Greg asked.

"She does not want to talk.
Not right now."

Months went by.
Hope was moved to the clinic.
Greg's parents drove to visit her.
They came back with more news.

"She is getting better," Greg's
dad said.

Greg wanted to know more.
But his dad did not talk much.
Greg asked his mom.

"Not much to say," she said.
"She will be home soon. And
she will need a lot of help."

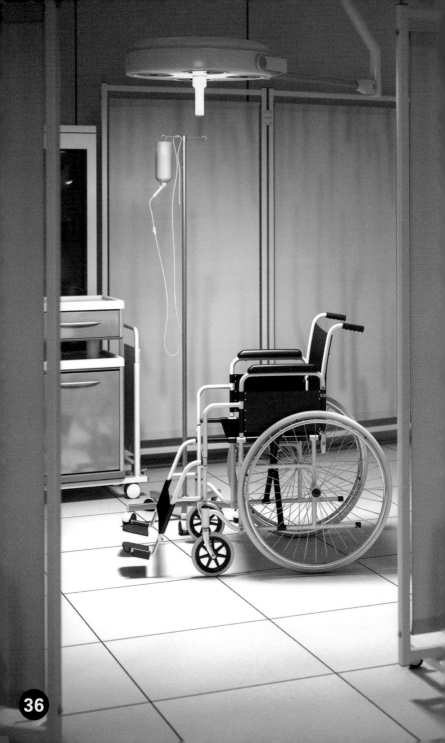

More months went by. Hope
still did not want to talk to him.
Greg stopped asking about her.
But he did not stop thinking
about her.

He wondered about her.
When would she come home?
What would she be like?

Greg waited at the window.
He had lost track of time.
Then he saw the car.
It was his mom and dad.
Hope was with them.

Greg could not move.
He could not speak.
He did not know
how to act.

Greg's dad got out.
He was smiling.
What did that mean?

Greg kept looking
out the window.
Where was Hope's
wheelchair?

Greg's dad walked around the car. He opened the car door. He helped Hope out.

She stood up.
Greg could not believe it.

Hope held on to her dad's arm.
She slowly walked to the house.
Greg ran to the front door.

Hope was walking!
She had a limp.
But she was walking.

Greg threw the door open. Hope smiled. Greg wanted to **hug her.** He was so happy. But he held back. He did not want to knock her down.

"You can walk!" Greg said. "But how?"

"Give me a hug first," Hope said.

"Be careful!" their mom said.

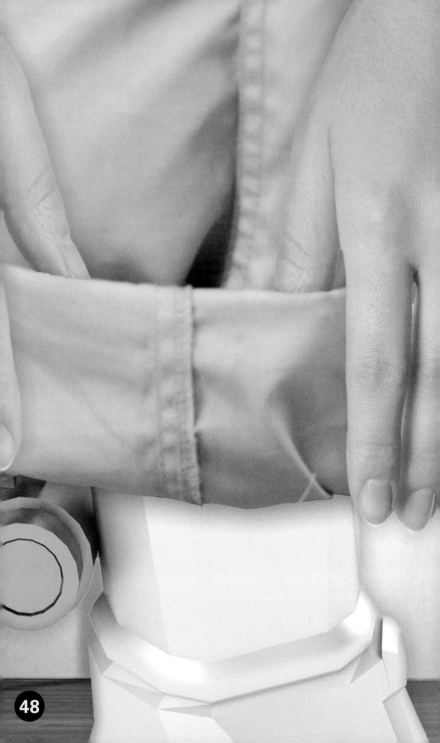

Greg and Hope hugged.
They all came into the house.

"But your leg," Greg said.
"They said that you lost it."

"I did," Hope said. "Part of it.
From the knee down.

Hope pulled up her pant leg.
"But now I have this."

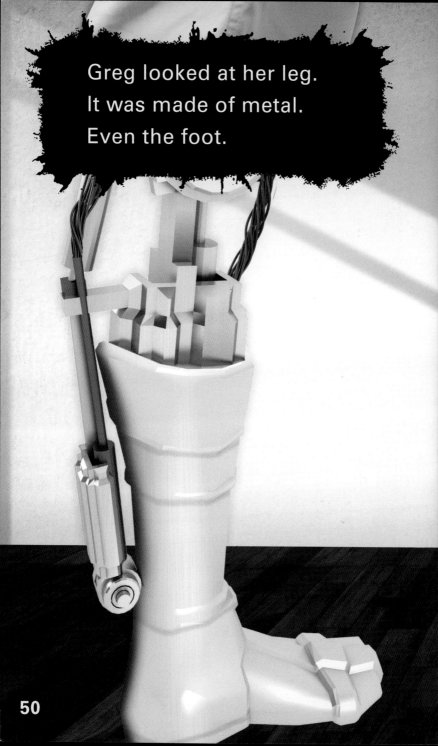

Greg looked at her leg.
It was made of metal.
Even the foot.

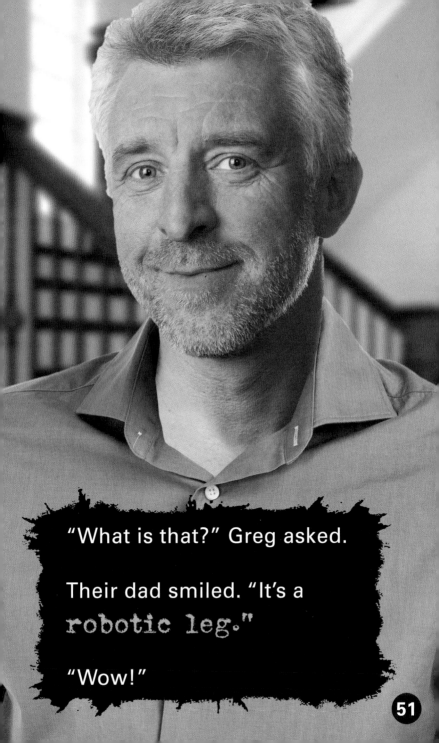

"What is that?" Greg asked.

Their dad smiled. "It's a robotic leg."

"Wow!"

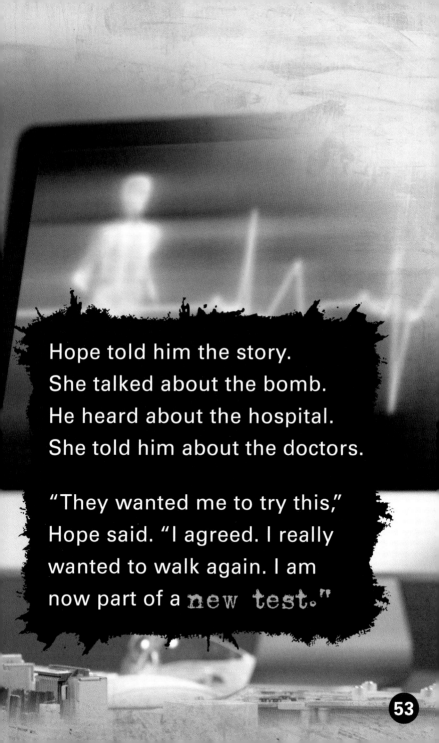

Hope told him the story.
She talked about the bomb.
He heard about the hospital.
She told him about the doctors.

"They wanted me to try this,"
Hope said. "I agreed. I really
wanted to walk again. I am
now part of a new test."

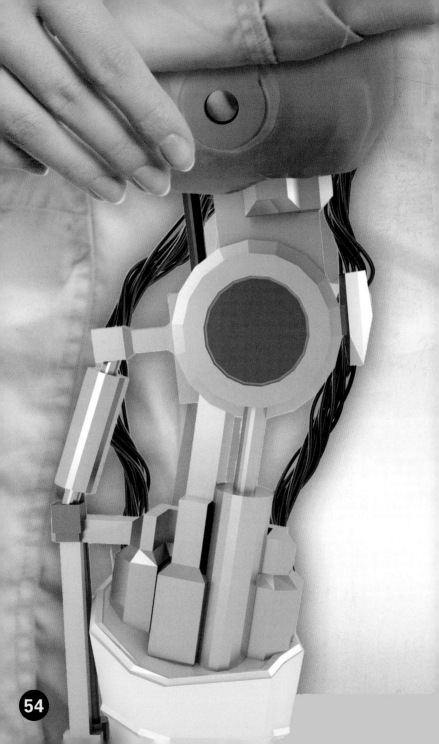

Hope showed Greg how her new leg worked. There was a cap on her knee.

"There are wires in my leg," she said. "They connect to the cap. The cap connects to the robotic leg."

"What do the wires do?" Greg asked.

"My brain tells my leg to move," said Hope. "That message goes into the wires."

"That makes your leg move?" Greg asked.

"Yes," Hope said. "It took me a long time to get used to it. It has been hard work. And I still have a long way to go. One day I will run again."

Hope had more news.
Her new hospital was only
an hour away.

"You're back for good?"
Greg asked.

"Yes," Hope said.

Greg stopped smiling.
"You never wanted to talk.
Why?"

"I know and I'm sorry,"
Hope said.

"We wanted to tell you," their mom said.

"About the new leg," their dad said.

"I told them not to," Hope said. "I wanted to tell you myself. And I wanted to show you."

Greg did not know what to say.

"We have a lot to talk about," Hope said.

Greg nodded his head.

"Hey," Hope said. "Where's my glove?"

"Your baseball glove?" Greg asked.

"Yes. Want to toss a few in the backyard?"

Greg smiled.

TEEN EMERGENT READER LIBRARIES®

BOOSTERS

The Literacy Revolution Continues with New TERL Booster Titles!

Each Sold Individually

ENGAGE [2]

9781680211146

9781680211337

9781680211290

9781680211535

9781680211313

EXCEL [3]

9781680211306

9781680211320

NEW TITLES COMING SOON!
www.jointheliteracyrevolution.com

TEEN EMERGENT READER LIBRARIES

Our *Teen Emergent Reader Libraries*® have been developed to solve the issue of motivating the most struggling teen readers to pick up a book and start reading. Written at the emergent and beginning reading levels, the books offer mature, teen-centric storylines that entice teens to read.

[1] EMERGE	[2] ENGAGE	[3] EXCEL

9781622508662	9781622508679	9781622508686

www.jointheliteracyrevolution.com